Acknowledge...

This book is dedicated to all the children I have read to and that have enjoyed my puppet shows. The joy I see on your faces brings joy to my heart.

To my mom and dad, thank you for always believing in me.

To my sister Brenda, I will always remember and cherish the good times we had together.

Rick Daniels

In the summer of 2016, Ike and Mike and all of their friends moved from the house on the 700th block of Jefferson Street North West, to their new home on the 600th block of Edgewood Street North East.

Their new home is no ordinary house either, in this house there is also magic! To make the magic begin, all you have to do is close your eyes and say,

*"COME TO LIFE, IKE!
COME TO LIFE, MIKE!"*

They will come alive in an amazing magical storybook adventure!

Published by Foxey World Publishing
Division of The Friends of Rick Daniels
635 Edgewood ST NE, Washington DC 20017
www.thefriendsofrickdaniels.com

Written by Rick Daniels
Illustrations by Denis Prouix
Edited by Derilyn Monconduit

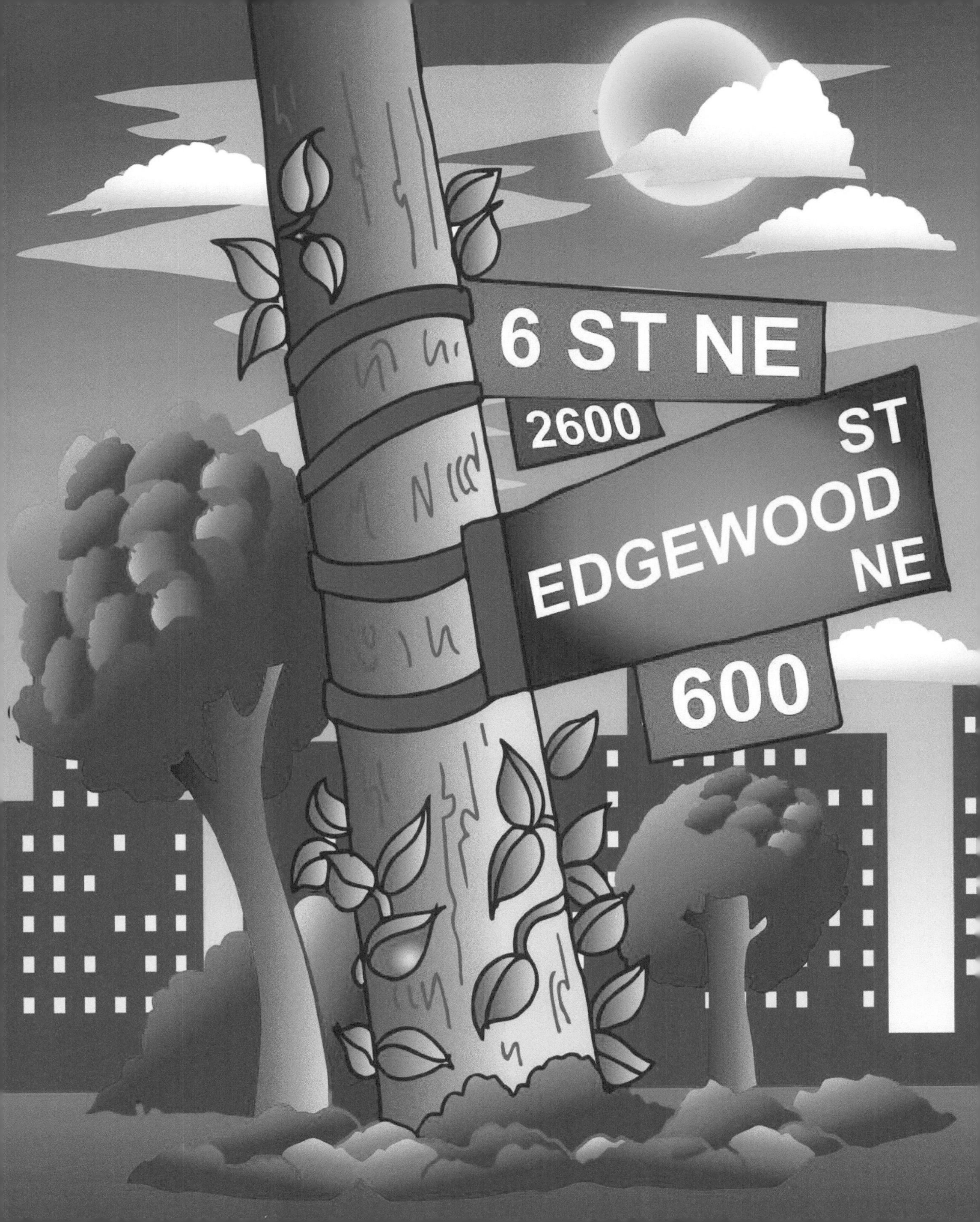
6 ST NE
2600
ST
EDGEWOOD
NE
600

Ever since Ike and Mike arrived at their new home on the 600th block of Edgewood Street North East, all they do is sit on the back of the sofa, with the rest of their animal friends.

One day Ike tells his older brother Mike, "I'm tired of sitting on this sofa! All we do is sit just like at Jefferson Street!"
Mike asks, "Well, what would you like to do today?"
Ike says, "I don't know."
Mike says, "We should go bowling!"
Ike asks, "What's bowling?"

Mike tells Ike, "You have to throw a ball down an alley and try to knock down all ten pins, that's called a strike.
We can go to Lucky Strike, a bowling alley at Gallery Place."
Ike asks, "How will we get there?"
Mike tells Ike, " We'll take the Red Line Metro train!"

The two put on their back packs and off they go! It's only a short walk from the house on Edgewood Street North East to the Red Line train station.

Once they're on the platform, a fast moving train comes barreling down the track!

Mike tells Ike, "COUNT THE CARS IKE! COUNT THE CARS! HOW MANY DO YOU SEE?"

As the the fast-moving train goes by, Ike counts,

"1,2,3,4,5"

He then says, "They're going too fast, I can't keep up."

Mike says, "You did great Ike!"

After a short ride, a voice comes over the loudspeaker, "Gallery Place! This is Chinatown!"

Mike says, "This is our stop, Ike!"

The two get off of the train and up the escalator they go.

Ike asks Mike, "Which way do we go? There are so many people, hold my hand! Mike, how do you know so much?"

Mike says, "It's because I am the oldest."

Ike says, "Yeah, only by one minute."

Mike says, "Well, that still makes me the oldest."

Not sure where to go, they ask a policeman for directions.

They say, "Hi Mr. Policeman! We're going bowling! Do you know the way to Lucky Strike?"

The policeman being a tiger says,

"ROAR! ROAR! ROAR!
it's in that building on the second floor."

Ike and Mike tell the policeman, "Thank you Mr. Policeman."

They find Lucky Strike and when they walk in a beautiful swan greets them.

Ike and Mike tell her "We would like to bowl."

The swan says, "Follow me, please."

Ike and Mike get their bowling shoes and they are ready to bowl.

Mike tells Ike, "Remember, if you knock down ten pins, it's called a strike."

Mike starts the game and throws the first ball.

Ike says, "I thought you were supposed to knock down ten pins, you only knocked down one."

Mike says, "I get a second chance!"

He throws the ball again and this time he knocks down one more pin.

Ike says, "You knocked down

$1 + 1 = 2$."

Ike says, "It's my turn!"

Ike throws the ball and knocks down two pins. He says, "I get a second chance!" Ike throws the ball again and this time he knocks down one more pin.

Mike says, "You knocked down

$$2+1=3."$$

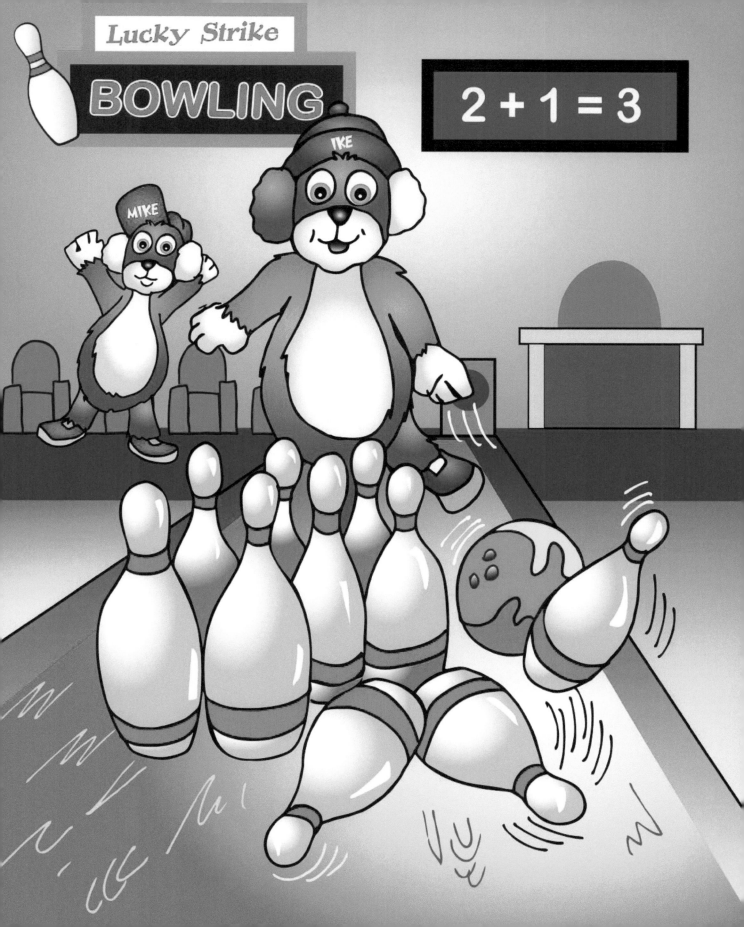

Mike says, "It's my turn!" Mike throws the ball and knocks down three pins." He says, "I get a second chance!" He throws the ball again and this time he knocks down one more pin.

Ike says, "You knocked down

3+1=4."

Ike says, "It's my turn!" Ike throws the ball and knocks down four pins. He says, "I get a second chance!" He throws the ball again and this time he knocks down one more pin.

Mike says, "You knocked down

4+1=5."

Mike says, "It's my turn!" Mike throws the ball and knocks down five pins. He says, "I get a second chance!" He throws the ball again and this time he knocks down one more pin.
Ike says, "You knocked down

$$5+1=6."$$

Ike says, "It's my turn!" Ike throws the ball and knocks down six pins."He says, "I get a second chance!" He throws the ball again and this time he knocks down one more pin.
Mike says, "You knocked down

6+1=7."

Mike says, "It's my turn!" Mike throws the ball and knocks down seven pins. He says, "I get a second chance!" He throws the ball again and this time he knocks down one more pin.

Ike says, "You knocked down

$$7+1=8.$$"

Ike says, "It's my turn!" Ike throws the ball and knocks down eight pins. He says, "I get a second chance!" He throws the ball again and this time he knocks down one more pin.

Mike says, "You knocked down

$$8+1=9."$$

8 + 1 = 9

Mike says, "It's my turn!" Mike throws the ball and knocks down nine pins. He says, "I get a second chance!" He throws the ball again and this time he knocks down one more pin.

Ike says, "You knocked down

$$9+1=10.\text{"}$$

9 + 1 = 10

Ike says, "Mike this took all day! The next time we go bowling, I have a better way, watch me!" Ike gets ready and throws the ball.

Mike hollers," Let the ball go, Ike! Let it go!"

Ike goes flying down the aisle with his fingers still stuck in the ball. He crashes into the pins and knocks them all down!

After a long day of bowling, Ike tells Mike, "I'm hungry."

Mike says, "Me too!"

Ike asks Mike, "Where can we go to eat?"

Mike suggests Carolina Kitchen. So, the two get back on the Red Line train. They get off at Rhode Island Station and it's only a short walk to Carolina Kitchen.

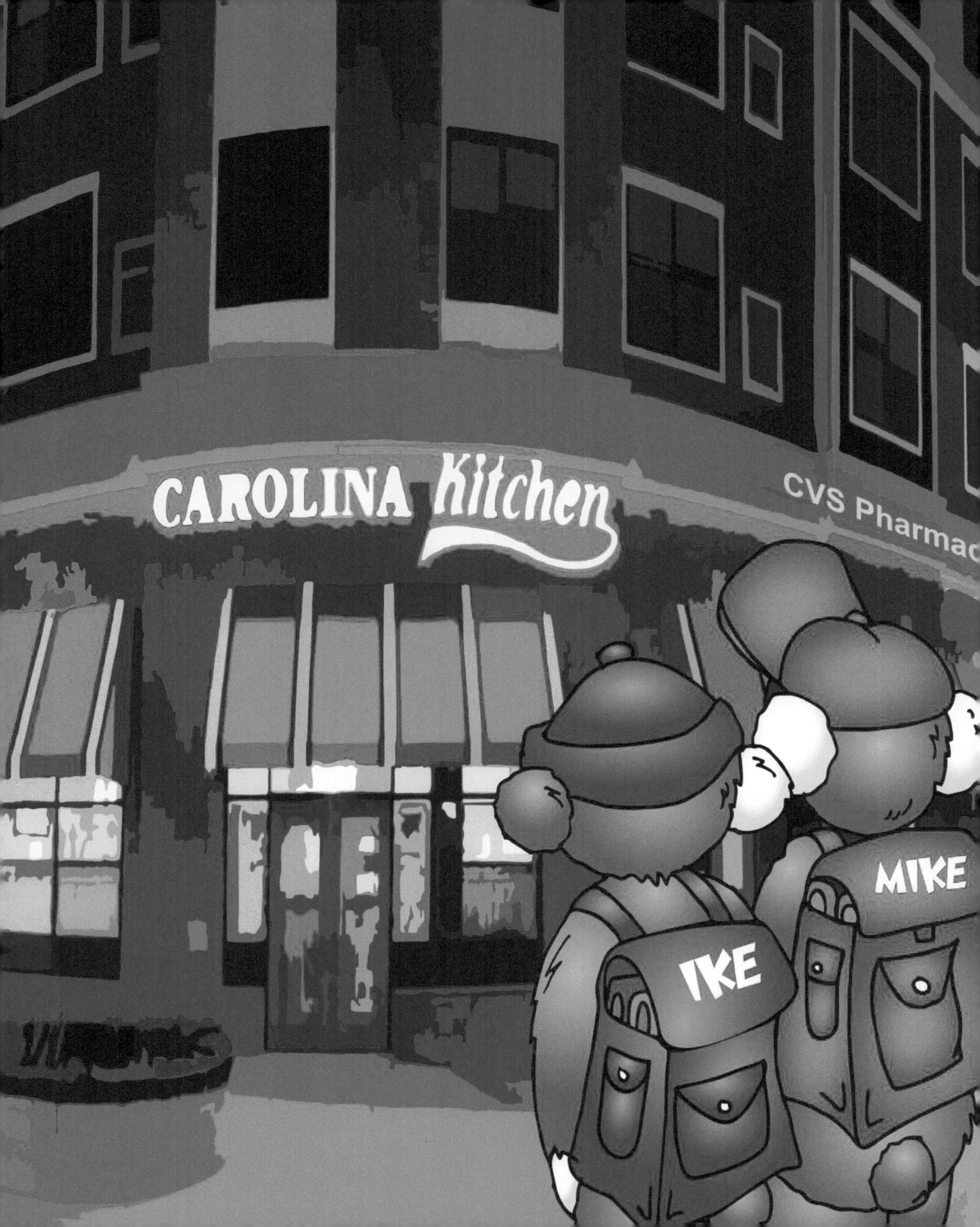
CAROLINA Kitchen
CVS Pharmac
MIKE
IKE

When they enter Carolina Kitchen, a beautiful peacock greets them, and says,

"Welcome! Welcome! Welcome!"

Ike tells her, "We're hungry."
She tells them, "You've come to the right place! Follow me and I will take you to a table." She seats them and says, "Your waitress will be right with you."

A pink flamingo comes over and asks them, "What would you to like to order?"

After looking over their menus, Mike tells her, "I'm going to have: BBQ ribs, mac-and-cheese, collard greens, candied yams, and potato salad. For dessert, I will have some peach cobbler with vanilla ice cream. Oh, and a glass of lemonade, please."

Ike says, "I will have the same please, except I would like fried chicken, and for dessert I will have sweet potato pie with vanilla ice cream, please."

The pink flamingo comes back with two plates full of food. Ike and Mike are so excited to eat after a long day of bowling.

She tells them, "Here's your food! I hope you enjoy it and let me know if there is anything else I can do for you."

After eating so much food, Ike and Mike fall asleep at the dinner table! They wake up and pay for their food. They only have a short walk back to their house on Edgewood Street North East.

Once they arrive to the house on the 600 Block of Edgewood Street North East, they take their place back on the sofa, with the rest of their animal friends.

   For now, the magic is over, but if you want another story just remember the secret! To make the magic begin, all you have do is close your eyes and say,

"Come to life Ike,
Come to like Mike!"

Until their next magical storybook adventue,

GOOD BYE!

Hi kids! We would like to introduce you to Ike and Mike's friends who sit on the back of the sofa with them.

There is Lucky, the yellow tiger cub, on the left.

Sabbie, the lion cub.

There are two tiger cubs,Temujin and his younger sister, Temuwae, and of course, Ike and Mike.

Each of their friends have their own books that will soon be released.

There is more magic and adventures on the way!

addition

1
1 + 1 = 2
2 + 1 = 3
3 + 1 = 4
4 + 1 = 5
5 + 1 = 6
6 + 1 = 7
7 + 1 = 8
8 + 1 = 9
9 + 1 = 10
10 + 1 = 11
11 + 1 = 12
12 + 1 = 13

2
1 + 2 = 3
2 + 2 = 4
3 + 2 = 5
4 + 2 = 6
5 + 2 = 7
6 + 2 = 8
7 + 2 = 9
8 + 2 = 10
9 + 2 = 11
10 + 2 = 12
11 + 2 = 13
12 + 2 = 14

3
1 + 3 = 4
2 + 3 = 5
3 + 3 = 6
4 + 3 = 7
5 + 3 = 8
6 + 3 = 9
7 + 3 = 10
8 + 3 = 11
9 + 3 = 12
10 + 3 = 13
11 + 3 = 14
12 + 3 = 15

4
1 + 4 = 5
2 + 4 = 6
3 + 4 = 7
4 + 4 = 8
5 + 4 = 9
6 + 4 = 10
7 + 4 = 11
8 + 4 = 12
9 + 4 = 13
10 + 4 = 14
11 + 4 = 15
12 + 4 = 16

5
1 + 5 = 6
2 + 5 = 7
3 + 5 = 8
4 + 5 = 9
5 + 5 = 10
6 + 5 = 11
7 + 5 = 12
8 + 5 = 13
9 + 5 = 14
10 + 5 = 15
11 + 5 = 16
12 + 5 = 17

6
1 + 6 = 7
2 + 6 = 8
3 + 6 = 9
4 + 6 = 10
5 + 6 = 11
6 + 6 = 12
7 + 6 = 13
8 + 6 = 14
9 + 6 = 15
10 + 6 = 16
11 + 6 = 17
12 + 6 = 18

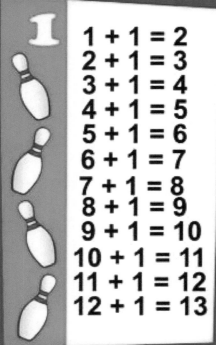
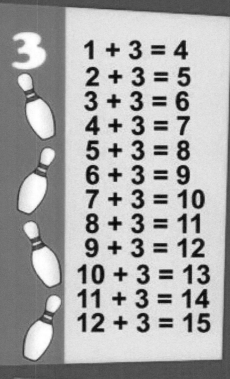
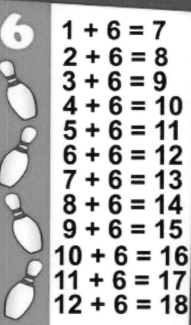

addition

7
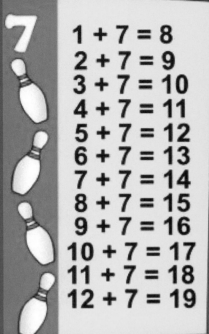

1 + 7 = 8
2 + 7 = 9
3 + 7 = 10
4 + 7 = 11
5 + 7 = 12
6 + 7 = 13
7 + 7 = 14
8 + 7 = 15
9 + 7 = 16
10 + 7 = 17
11 + 7 = 18
12 + 7 = 19

8

1 + 8 = 9
2 + 8 = 10
3 + 8 = 11
4 + 8 = 12
5 + 8 = 13
6 + 8 = 14
7 + 8 = 15
8 + 8 = 16
9 + 8 = 17
10 + 8 = 18
11 + 8 = 19
12 + 8 = 20

9

1 + 9 = 10
2 + 9 = 11
3 + 9 = 12
4 + 9 = 13
5 + 9 = 14
6 + 9 = 15
7 + 9 = 16
8 + 9 = 17
9 + 9 = 18
10 + 9 = 19
11 + 9 = 20
12 + 9 = 21

10

1 + 10 = 11
2 + 10 = 12
3 + 10 = 13
4 + 10 = 14
5 + 10 = 15
6 + 10 = 16
7 + 10 = 17
8 + 10 = 18
9 + 10 = 19
10 + 10 = 20
11 + 10 = 21
12 + 10 = 22

11

1 + 11 = 12
2 + 11 = 13
3 + 11 = 14
4 + 11 = 15
5 + 11 = 16
6 + 11 = 17
7 + 11 = 18
8 + 11 = 19
9 + 11 = 20
10 + 11 = 21
11 + 11 = 22
12 + 11 = 23

12

1 + 12 = 13
2 + 12 = 14
3 + 12 = 15
4 + 12 = 16
5 + 12 = 17
6 + 12 = 18
7 + 12 = 19
8 + 12 = 20
9 + 12 = 21
10 + 12 = 22
11 + 12 = 23
12 + 12 = 24

CPSIA information can be obtained
at www.ICGtesting.com
Printed in the USA
BVHW02n0128201018
530732BV00005B/34/P

* 9 7 8 0 6 9 2 1 2 8 9 5 4 *